There Was an Old Martian Who Swallowed the Moon

by Jennifer Ward

illustrated by Steve Gray

two lions

two lions

Published by Two Lions, New York
www.apub.com
Amazon, the Amazon logo, and Two Lions are trademarks of
Amazon.com, Inc., or its affiliates.
LCCN: 2014946858
ISBN-13: 9781477826287
ISBN-10: 1477826289
The illustrations are rendered in digital media.
Book design by Vera Soki
Printed in China
First Edition

For Hudson—J.W.
To my buddy Tom Knight—S.G.

There was an old Martian . . .

... who swallowed the moon.
With a dish and a spoon,
he dined on the moon.

I don't know why he swallowed the moon.

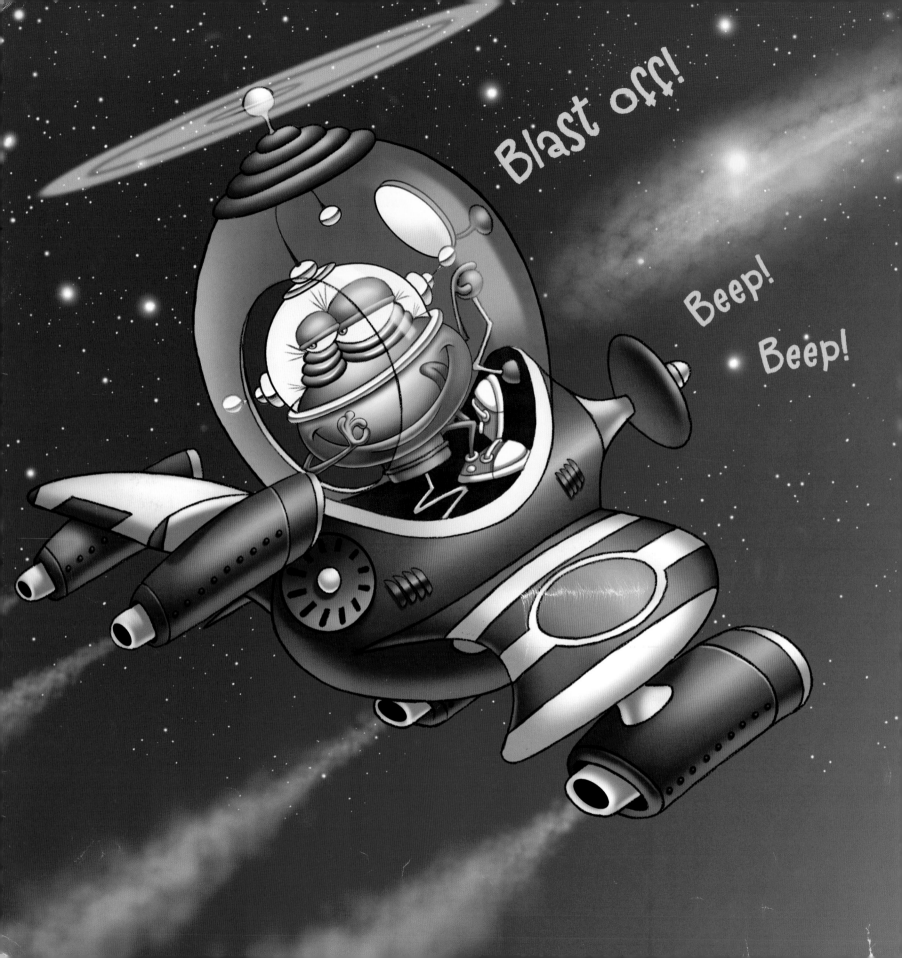

There was
an old Martian
who swallowed a cow.

Don't ask me how
he swallowed
that cow.

He swallowed the cow right after the moon.

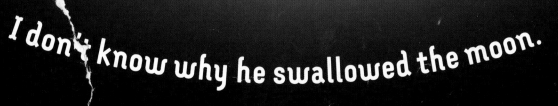

I don't know why he swallowed the moon.

Blast off!

Beep!

Beep!

There was an old Martian
who swallowed a comet.
He zipped down on it—
then swallowed that comet.

ZOOM!

He swallowed the comet right after the cow.
He swallowed the cow right after the moon.

I don't know why he swallowed the moon.

There was an old Martian . . .

ZOOM!

There was an old Martian . . .

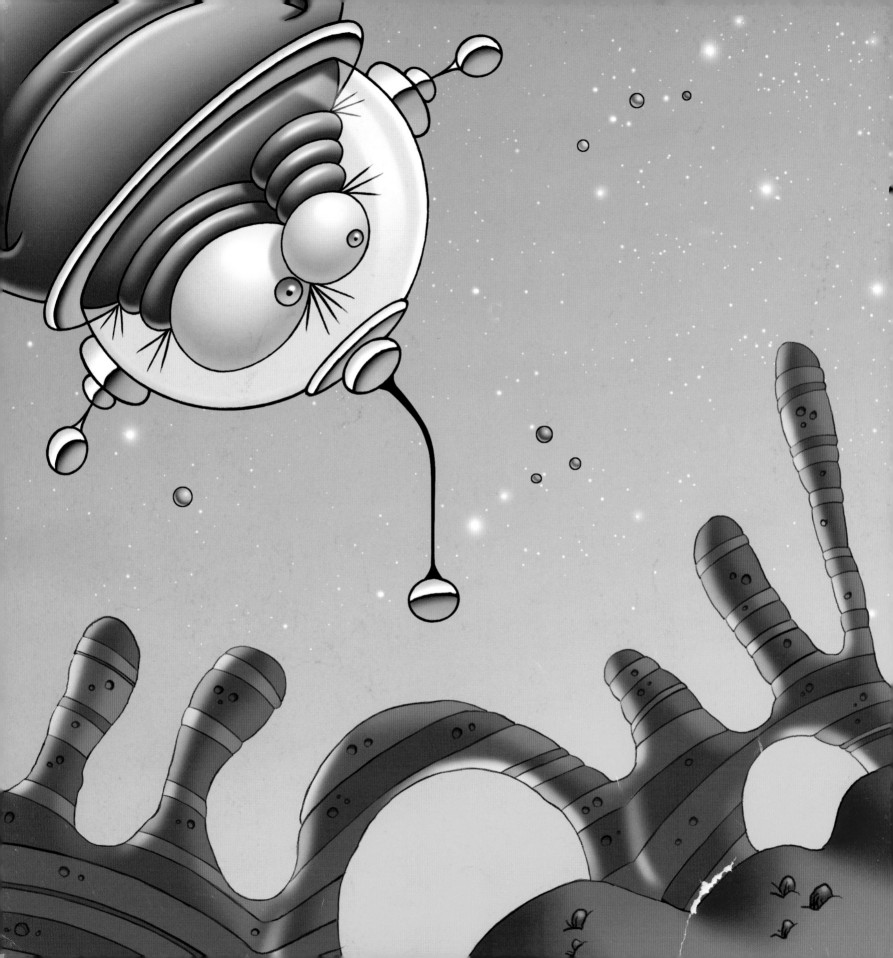

. . . who swallowed a rover.

Exploration was over
for that busy rover.

He swallowed the rover right after the ship.
He swallowed the ship right after the comet.
He swallowed the comet right after the cow.
He swallowed the cow right after the moon.
I don't know why he swallowed the moon.

There was an old Martian...

... who swallowed Mars.
It made him see stars to gobble up Mars!

He swallowed Mars right after the rover.
He swallowed the rover right after the ship.
He swallowed the ship right after the comet.
He swallowed the comet right after the cow.
He swallowed the cow right after the moon.

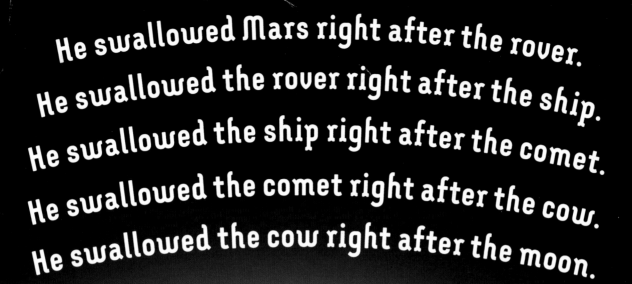

I don't know why he swallowed the moon.

There was an old Martian . . .

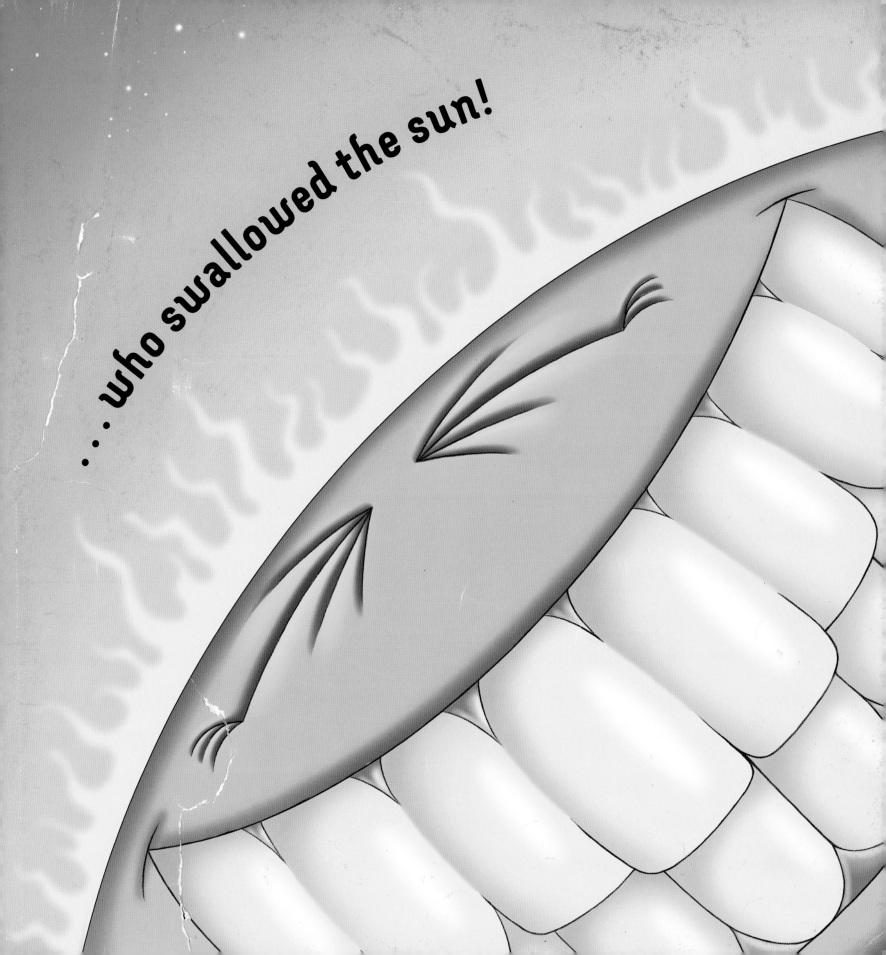

This Martian is done!